STO

The
Manifesto
& me
– Meg

The Manifesto & me –Meg

Bobbi Katz

Franklin Watts, Inc.
1974
New York

Design by Rafael Hernandez

Library of Congress Cataloging in Publication Data
Katz, Bobbi.
  The manifesto and me–Meg.

  SUMMARY: Sixth-grader Meg is unprepared for the
events that follow her decision to organize a consciousness-raising group to learn more about the principles
of women's liberation.
  [1. Women's rights—Fiction] I. Title.
PZ7.I57Man   [Fic]   74-4205
ISBN 0-531-02739-2

1825083

For my "Saturday Sisters":
Kate, Barbara, and Morag

1

MOSTLY IT'S A BETTER deal if you get to be born a boy. That's why I'm a Women's Libber.

My Aunt Francie says the Women Libbers are crazy. She says girls get to have a lot of pretty clothes and fancy jewelry, and men should open the door for them and a whole lot of other junk.

"I don't need anyone to call me Ms.!" That's what Aunt Francie says. "I'm happy being Mrs. Mark Graham. I don't want any man's job."

When I was little, I used to think Aunt Francie was just wonderful. She always smelled terrific, like the perfume counter in a department store. Her clothes were always perfect, and her hair was always perfect. She wore lipstick all the time and even showed me how to put it on. You have to do it with this little brush, carefully like you're gluing a model airplane together.

I used to wish my Mom was like Aunt Francie, instead of clonking around in blue jeans after work with her hair in pigtails.

I don't know why I keep saying "was" and "were." Aunt Francie hasn't really changed much, except that now her hair is blond. I guess maybe what's changed is me.

One time when Mom had to go to some conference, I got to stay at Aunt Francie's house for a week. She had me all psyched up about the neat things we were going to do in the city like see the dinosaurs and go to the zoo and visit department stores. Well, we did get to see an awful lot of department stores. I even got a little bored with riding in elevators and going up and down the escalators. But Aunt Francie always was too exhausted to go to see the dinosaurs or in a rush to get to a beauty parlor appointment or a cooking lesson.

That is another thing about Aunt Francie. She takes these cooking lessons that "cost a fortune," and she "can't afford to miss one." Wouldn't you think she'd be a fantastic cook? No way! Not Aunt Francie. She's always racing around before my uncle comes home, pulling stuff out of the freezer. She clunks these steaks, frozen like rocks, under the water faucet. She starts tossing plastic bags into pans, defrosts a pie and whammo! Supper!

Well anyway, I don't think Aunt Francie is so wonderful anymore. She's O.K., but I'm glad she's not my Mom. I mean you can't really depend on her.

Anyhow, whenever she gets together with my mother lately, they get in this big hassle. My Mom is a doctor. Not the kind like you get sick and go to their office and get a shot kind. She's a just-for-ladies doctor. She doesn't have a real office. She works at the clinic in the Centerville Hospital. She usually gets home just before I do, unless there is some enormous emergency.

Anyhow, Mom and I were just relaxing over a cup of coffee, after school and work. It's dopey, but that's kind of my favorite time of the day. Mom tells me how things went for her. I tell her what happened at school. Mom likes it, too. She even takes the phone off the hook. It's our private time.

Just as we settled down, in bombed Aunt Francie. Aunt Francie doesn't live around the corner. It takes almost an hour to get here from her house. We were surprised to see her.

Wow! Was she fuming! She had planned a big, fancy dinner party with all the right people "just to help" us. She thought she was doing something wonderful.

"After I spent weeks nourishing the Littlewoods, telling them about my brilliant brother and what a fabulous architect he was, you didn't show up. No phone call. No excuses. Nothing!"

"Oh, Francie," Mom said. "I'm so sorry. I've been all wrapped up thinking about an operation that was scheduled this morning. I just forgot."

"Forgot!" said Aunt Francie. "I spent weeks planning that dinner, just so John could meet the Littlewoods. I spent weeks convincing them that John was just the architect to design their new house, and *you* forgot! If you were home being a proper mother, helping your husband with his career, you wouldn't forget. John wouldn't be designing rinky–dink houses and churches that look like barns. He'd be a success, raking in money. But no! You have to go on playing Dr. Ms. It wouldn't surprise me if poor Meg here ended up being some kind of juvenile delinquent, the way you neglect her. Neglect! That's how kids turn out to be dope addicts, unmarried mothers. Look at her! Eleven years old and drinking coffee."

Right then and there, I decided one thing for sure. No matter what, I'm not going to be a juvenile delinquent. I'll show Aunt Francie how wrong she was! Besides, I think taking dope is dumb, really dumb. That's why they call it dope. I don't want to be an unmarried mother either. With all the homework Mrs. Martin gives us, I have enough books to drag around without having to lug a baby.

"Francie, I'm sorry about your party, really sorry," Mom said. "But you're wrong about John and Meg, too. My working gives John some freedom to design homes that interest him."

Then Aunt Francie said this, and Mom said that. Back and forth and back and forth.

Then all of a sudden Aunt Francie looked at her watch. "Good grief, look at the time!" she said. "I've got Bowling League tonight!"

"Don't forget, Meg. Come spend a weekend. We'll do marvelous things!" she said and gave me a quick kiss.

I could still smell her perfume, while I helped Mom wash the coffee cups.

"Mom," I said. "Could I join one of those con-sciousness-raising groups, the kind you're always saying Aunt Francie should?"

Mom looked at me, half smiling. She wiped Aunt Francie's lipstick off my forehead extra care-fully.

"I don't think there are any consciousness-raising groups for kids," she said. "But that's no reason you and some of your friends couldn't start one."

2

SAMANTHA MAHAN IS the kind of person you just have to admire, even if you don't like her. She can beat up any kid in the whole school, including McKinley Collins. She's kind of like Robin Hood. If anyone is picking on some little kid, whacko! She zaps him.

Sam doesn't get very good grades, but she is the best living artist I know.

When I called her, I tried to explain about getting a consciousness group going. Sam didn't get it at first. But when I mentioned stuff like girls not having a chance to get on the football team, she got it all right.

We decided to have a meeting at my house on Thursday right after school. Sam said she would make the posters.

One thing about Sam, you can depend on her. Anyone coming into school just had to see that poster. It had a big skull and crossbones and said WIPE OUT BOYS in purple, green, and orange letters. "Meeting Thursday at Meg Prescott's house, sharply after school."

I didn't think the words were so great, but it was a beautiful poster.

Everyone was buzzing about it and asking me questions, until the second bell rang and we took out our workbooks. People kept sending me notes, and I was so busy answering them that I didn't know the place when Mrs. Martin called on me.

It's no use trying to fudge around with Mrs. Martin. I felt my face get hot and my hands get that cold sticky feeling.

"Perhaps in the future, Meg, you will pay more attention to trying to wipe out the F I have just written next to your name in my grade book."

Some of the boys clapped.

I saw Shawn Higgins just sitting there with this kind of funny look on his face. When I was little and thought everybody had to get married, I was going to marry Shawn. I still really like him.

All morning I had been feeling so important. Now I didn't feel so important anymore.

I kept my eyes on my book, but Mrs. Martin didn't call on me again.

At lunchtime I had so much explaining to do that I couldn't even finish my egg salad sandwich. It's hard to explain about something like Women's Lib when you don't understand about it very much yourself.

A lot of kids said they would come to the meeting.

Sam told me she had put up posters at the delicatessen and George's. George's is this store that sells newspapers and candy and just about everything. Everybody in town goes there sooner or later.

Sam said she put my phone number on the posters, in case anyone wanted more information. I kind of hoped no one would have a pencil to write it down.

I mean, I wanted to have the consciousness-raising group and everything, but it was getting to be kind of like when I wanted a puppy. When you want a dog, you don't think about having to walk it when you don't want to or having to clean up the messes it makes on the floor. But later you can't just take the dog back to where you got it and say, "Sorry. I changed my mind."

3

DURING PRIVATE TIME
with Mom, I told her about how the kids were interested and everything. I left out the part about
what the poster said and the business with Mrs.
Martin.

Even before supper, the phone started ringing.
David answered it before anyone else got a
chance, but it was always for me. There were teasing calls from boys. There were calls from girls who
went to St. Mary's that I didn't even know. I just
told everyone to come to the meeting and I'd explain things then.

I felt really bad about all the phone calls because of what had happened with David last
month. Suzy, she's my best friend, and I were pretending David was an international criminal. It
wasn't hard to pretend. He's always locking himself up in his room with his radio playing loud. I
mean, he could have been building a bomb in
there or something. He's studying German and

Spanish in high school, which could be pretty handy for an international spy to know, too.

Before long Suzy and I were sneaking around following him. We kind of convinced ourselves he was an honest-to-goodness criminal. We had lots of clues but no real evidence.

There was only one thing to do. I would have to go through his desk.

That's kind of the biggest NO in our house. I mean, I'd DIE if I thought that anyone was poking around in my desk. A person has to have some private place.

On the other hand, what if he was really planning to blow up the whole country or hijack an airplane or something?

One day when Mom was coming home late, I had my chance. All that was in there were some empty chewing gum wrappers, junk like rulers and broken pencils, and these poems.

David had been writing poems! Mushy ones! They were all about this girl, Dorothy, I didn't even know. I copied one called "Math Class" about how the bonds of love were tied in his stomach when sunlight fell across her face, "turning each blemish into a gleaming star." It was the creepiest thing I ever read!

I thought it would be a great idea to kind of spring that poem at dinner, like I had just heard it. Wow! Was that ever a mistake!

David just looked at me. All these different feelings flickered over his face like when you try to fix the picture on the T.V. set.

I thought he was going to cry, but he didn't. He didn't say a word. He just gave me this awful look. He went up to his room and slammed the door real hard. We could hear his radio blaring all the way downstairs.

Mom and Dad didn't say anything. They didn't have to. I just sat there watching my ice cream melt and feeling like a rat.

Anyhow, I try not to tie up the phone when David's home. It's like he's waiting for someone, someone very special, to call him. I really don't think that whoever it is will ever call. But I figure that maybe he'll know how sorry I am, if I just don't use the phone when he's home.

And now *this!*

4

BY THE TIME DAD came home, my stomach was jumping. I mean, this wasn't like trying to sell your ice skates. I never got so many phone calls in my life!

When we sat down at the table, Dad said, "I understand there's going to be a meeting here on Thursday. I saw quite an impressive poster when I picked up the newspaper."

About the only bad thing about my father is that you're never quite sure when he's putting you on and when he isn't.

I guess the look I gave my mother spelled HELP because she said, "Meg is going to get a few girls together for a consciousness-raising group. I think it's a good thing."

"Consciousness-raising group!" my father said. "From the poster it sounded as if Meg was planning a blood bath! It said something like 'Do you want to murder boys? Come to Meg Prescott's house, Thursday after school.' Then it gave a phone number but not ours."

Even David, who usually tunes us out, was paying attention now.

"I understand that the poster in the delicatessen had a dagger dripping with blood and somewhat the same message," Dad said. "Some consciousness-raising group!" Half smiling, Dad got very busy cutting his meat.

Oh, Sam, why do you have to be so dependable? I kept wishing it was yesterday.

"That's all I need," said David. "That's really all I need! When Sherlock Holmes here isn't snooping through my stuff, she's off making a cretin of herself in front of the whole town. Every kid at Valley High will know I've got this dopey girl cretin sister. Great. Thanks, cretin!"

"Cretin" must be the new word on David's vocabulary list. He'll use it up by the end of the week.

"How does the defense plead, Meg?" Mom asked.

Mashed potatoes were sticking in my throat like lumps of cement. I sloshed down some milk.

"Well, see, I talked to Samantha Mahan about starting the group, and she made the posters because she's this great artist and everything. I guess she got a little carried away."

"How many posters are there, Meg?" my mother asked.

"Oh, just three," I said. "One at the deli, one at George's, and one at school."

"Just three!" David squeaked. Mostly his voice is low like a foghorn, but every once in a

14

while it comes out real high. "By now every single person in town has seen one of them!"

"By the way, dear," said Mom to my father, "the phone has been pretty hot around here all afternoon. You didn't happen to notice whose number was on the poster?"

"Well," said my father. "Here's a riddle for you. When people make a mistake dialing our number, what warmhearted, affectionate person do they usually reach?"

Oh, no! It was like in cartoons, when a light bulb goes on in someone's head. Except it wasn't a cartoon. It was my family, and that light bulb went on for all of us. One name was written on it in capital letters, and we could all read it: ABIGAIL WITHERSPOON!

Abigail Witherspoon, superintendent of schools for the whole county, president of the anti-alcohol league, and the crabbiest lady in the world!

Then a smaller light bulb went on. I hoped I was the only one who could see that one.

Dad really wanted to get the contract to design the new Woodbury Central Elementary School. He had come up with a fantastic design and had already turned in what they call a rendering and a preliminary plan. That means that he did this terrific drawing of how the school would look from the outside. He even stuck in the grass and trees. Then he did some drawings of how it would look to a giant, if he took off the roof and looked down at it.

Other architects were submitting their ideas, and the school board would choose the best. Naturally, we were all rooting for Dad. I mean, his was so good it had to be the best.

The school board would choose, but guess who would have the last word?

I felt Sin's cold nose against my ankle. He smelled so good that I had named him "My Sin" after Aunt Francie's perfume, but nobody ever bothered with the "My." I wished he was still a puppy and I had his messes to clean up, instead of this one.

5

MOM SAYS THAT WHEN-
ever you have a bunch of things to do, you should
do the hardest thing first. I guess she's right, but
I'm not very good at doing things that way. That's
why I decided to take the posters down before I
called Miss Witherspoon.

The window at George's was so full of posters
and announcements that I knocked down three of
them when I tried to get ours down. I couldn't get
over the way Sam had painted the blood. It looked
so real I was almost sure it would drip all over me.

George's was full of people, and George himself was behind the counter.

"What's the matter, Meg?" he asked. "Did you
decide to let the boys live, after all?"

I tried to explain that I was only trying to form
a kids' Women's Lib group. That really broke him
up. I could hear him laughing with the customers
halfway down the block.

At the deli, things were quiet. There was only

this high school kid waiting on customers, and there was only one customer.

"Hey," he said. "You're not David Prescott's little sister, are you?"

I wished I had taken my wallet with me. I've got this card in it a lady gave me at the airport. It says, "I am a deaf mute." On the back it has all the letters of the alphabet in sign language. What a perfect opportunity to use it!

I just tried to look deaf and dumb and got out of there as fast as I could.

Wow! If that was the easy part, what was calling Miss Witherspoon going to be like?

By the time I got home, David had gone off to a music lesson. Dad was at a meeting somewhere, and Mom was in the kitchen reading a medical journal.

Mom gave me a "squug" and asked to see the posters. A squug is kind of halfway between a squeeze and a hug. Mostly a squug makes you feel great, but this time that squug was all I needed. These dumb old tears started dripping down my face.

"Hey, Meg," Mom said. "Things aren't that bad, are they?"

No words would come out, so I just stayed there with Mom's arms around me like some little kid crybaby. I felt so mixed up and miserable, like after a nightmare.

When I thought about the mess I was in, I just wanted to stay there in Mom's arms forever. It was bad enough being in trouble with Mrs. Martin, but

Shawn Higgins probably thought I hated him, which is an absolute lie. My own brother thought I was a dopey girl cretin. He'd probably cremate me if his friends started teasing him about me in school. But the worst, the absolute worst, was that by getting all tangled up with Miss Abigail Witherspoon, I had probably ruined Dad's chances to get the Woodbury job. I mean she's so crabby, it wouldn't surprise me one bit to see her fly by with a cat on a broomstick.

Then this funny picture flashed through my mind. I could see the years go by and Mom and me getting to be old ladies with white hair and wrinkles, still sitting in the kitchen, squuging away. I knew then I had to start getting it all together.

It was as if Mom had seen the very same picture. She kind of mopped up my face with a napkin and smiled.

"Sam's posters are really something else," she said. "Sam is so angry at boys that she didn't say anything about consciousness-raising. Boys aren't the enemy. You know that, don't you, Meg?"

"But, Mom," I said. "If boys aren't the enemy, who is?"

"I guess you could say society or western civilization or something else that's so big that nobody could even begin to cope with it. But the number one enemy that a person can cope with is her head. That's what consciousness-raising groups are about—making you conscious of attitudes towards being a female you might not even know you had."

"But, Mom," I said. "Where do we start? All of

these kids are supposed to come to the meeting on Thursday. Some of them, like Sam, really have it in for boys, but most of them—I don't know what most of them want."

"Remember the rhyme, 'What Are Little Girls Made Of'?"

"Sure." I mean who doesn't know that song! "Sugar and spice and everything nice."

"That might be a good way to start. I don't think you'll need me," Mom added. "But I'll be back in the wings, just in case."

I really began to feel better. I guess I've got the best mother in the world, even if I forget sometimes.

"Now go call Suzy," Mom said. "See if she can come over after school tomorrow to help us make some cookies for your Thursday gang."

I called Suzy, but she couldn't come over. She said if I came to her house, her grandmother would help us make fortune cookies. Neato! We could write all the messages!

"Now, Meg, I think you better call Miss Witherspoon," Mom said.

I could tell from the tone in her voice that I wasn't going to be able to talk her into doing it for me.

6

I WENT OVER WHAT I was going to say to Miss Witherspoon a half a dozen times. I even brushed my teeth and used mouthwash, just in case. I dialed the number carefully, getting the fours and the ones in the right places and hoping that maybe the line was busy or she wasn't home. But no luck!

Have you ever gulped down a glass of cold lemonade without tasting to see if there was sugar in it? That's how Miss Witherspoon came on—like sour, cold lemonade.

"This is not Meg Prescott nor am I in any way interested in affecting the male population of this area," said the voice that answered.

I mean, she didn't even say "Hello" or anything! I just blurted out what I was going to say to her:

"Miss Witherspoon, this is Meg Prescott calling. I'd like to apologize for any inconvenience you may have been caused by the similarities in our phone numbers." The words came out like a locomotive chugging down the track.

"Inconvenience indeed! Miss Prescott, you have completely ruined my evening. Your colleagues have plagued me with phone calls, stopping my work and ruining my digestion."

"I'm really awfully sorry, Miss Witherspoon," I said. "I guess my friend was so excited about the meeting, she didn't take the time to check my phone number when she made the poster."

"I can only wonder what sort of parents would allow young women to hold such meetings like a band of hoodlums."

Oh, wow! I couldn't let her think that!

"But Miss Witherspoon, Sam, she's my friend who made the posters, doesn't understand too much about Women's Liberation. It's my fault for not helping her make them that they came out so bloody and the phone numbers got mixed up and everything."

"Miss Prescott, in the words of the immortal Matthew Arnold, 'Look to your English.' Your use of language is deplorable. Meanwhile, please explain what your meeting has to do with Women's Liberation."

If I looked to my English, I wouldn't be able to explain anything. I decided to explain now and look later.

"Well, Women's Lib has consciousness-raising groups, but there aren't any for kids," I said. "Mom said we could start one and that's what the meeting's about."

I just let that old preposition dangle there and hoped Miss Witherspoon wouldn't notice. Her voice changed, maybe half a teaspoon of sugar's worth. "A consciousness-raising group? What grade are you in, Miss Prescott?"

"Sixth," I answered, wishing she would just call me "Meg." I mean, nobody ever calls me "Miss."

"Don't you think that consciousness-raising is premature for girls your age?" she asked.

One thing about talking on the telephone is even if you don't want to talk, there are these awful silences that are worse than having what you want to say come out wrong. I knew I just had to try and explain.

"I'm worried that if we wait until we grow up, a lot of kids will grow up wrong. I mean they'll be stuck being one kind of people, when maybe they could have been a more themselves kind."

Old Miss Witherspoon wasn't saying anything, so I just slogged on. It would have been nice if somebody rang her doorbell or something, but nobody did.

"Like Suzy, my best friend, she knows she wants to be a detective. She even has these cards we printed all ready to go that say 'Suzy Suong, Private Eye, No Case Too Hard to Crack.' But if she didn't know for sure, she might end up being an airplane stewardess or the lady that passes out the menus in the Chinese restaurant. Especially with people always saying girls can't do this and girls can't do that. But all the time, deep down, she'd be missing something."

"I think I understand what you mean, Meg. I may call you Meg, may I not?"

Miss Witherspoon was beginning to sound human. But just when I was beginning to think, well, maybe she's not so bad, she wiped me out.

"I'd like to join your group, perhaps as an adult adviser," she said.

Adult adviser? What kid wants some grown-up bossing her around? I mean between parents and teachers we get enough advice! And Miss Witherspoon, she's not even an adult! She's an antique.

"Sure. That would be great," I lied. Ever since Dad read me *Pinocchio* when I was real little, I've had this dumb habit of running my finger along my nose to check if it's growing when I tell a lie. I was nearly rubbing it off!

I know I was being a real phony and all, but what would you have said to Miss Abigail Witherspoon? What would you have said?

7

PARENTS ARE REALLY
unpredictable people. Like if you expect to really
catch it for doing something horrible, they just say,
"Don't let it happen again" or "Try harder" or
something like that.

I never expected my mother to laugh when I
told her about Miss Witherspoon, but she did. It
really broke her up. Hah, hah. Big joke!

My Dad didn't think it was all that funny that
Miss Witherspoon wanted to join our group. But he
didn't think it was all that bad either. He told me
stuff about Miss Witherspoon that made me think
twice.

Like did you know she's just about the highest
paid person in the whole county? If she wanted to,
she could make people call her "Doctor" because
she has a Ph.D., which means Doctor of Philosophy. When she got her doctorate, which was about
a million years ago, there were hardly any women
that did. I mean, it was way before Women's Lib.
It was when almost everyone thought that girls

shouldn't do anything but look pretty so they could catch a husband and have a lot of babies. It's hard enough being a Women's Libber now, but can you imagine what it was like for her? I mean, it was practically the Dark Ages, when Miss Witherspoon was young.

I was feeling a lot better about Miss Witherspoon and everything else by the time I left for school Wednesday morning. I kind of have this thing about really gutsy people. I just really like them, even if they have terrible personalities. I just wished I didn't taste sour lemonade every time I thought about A.W. But if she turned some kids off, well, that wasn't so bad. I mean she had really kind of earned the right.

Wednesday morning was one of those days you just had to feel happy people come with noses. I don't wear glasses or anything you need a nose for, but the world just smelled so good—clear and fresh and just a little bit cold.

People aren't allowed to burn leaves in our town. It's a rule. There were big piles of leaves that people had raked into the gutter for the town truck to pick up. It was nice to crunch through them.

I met Suzy halfway to school. We walked together, crunching through the leaves and not talking much. It's great to have a friend like Suzy who feels like talking when you feel like talking and feels like being quiet just when you do.

When we got to school, there was Sam right outside the door. She was fuming mad because someone had taken our poster down. She was kind of giving everyone the once-over as they went in. She was sure McKinley Collins had taken it down and was all psyched up to cremate him.

I guess I saved that kid at least a black eye because I told Sam I had to talk to her. I told her about having to take the other posters down and the mix-up with the phone numbers and Miss Witherspoon and all that. Old McKinley just walked into school like a lamb while we were talking.

Sam was getting mad at me. I explained that the posters were really great and everything but kind of gave the wrong impression. When I said the main thing about consciousness-raising wasn't to get boys, she really blew her stack.

"If you think I want to be in some dumb girls' club and sit around with dumb girls and their dumb Taffy Teen Dolls, you're bats," Sam said.

I tried to explain that wasn't what I wanted to do either, but she just stomped off. Sam is one of those people who see things all black or all white. She doesn't understand about in-betweens.

When I got upstairs to Mrs. Martin's room, all I got to do was hang up my jacket because Mrs. Martin said Mr. Baker, the principal, wanted to see me in his office.

How can it be that a day can start out so peaceful and quiet and all of a sudden turn into a mess?

MR. BAKER IS NOT A
bad guy, considering he is a principal and all
that. Sometimes when I'm fishing at Riley's Pond,
he's fishing, too. He always waves or says "Hello"
or something, but he doesn't get into some big conversation and spook the fish away like some grown-
ups would. But getting called to his office, that was
different. I mean he wasn't calling me into his office to talk about trout lures or night crawlers.

His secretary said to go right in, so I did. I
would have felt better if he had been wearing his
mashed-up fishing hat, but of course he wasn't. He
was puffing on his pipe, just like he always did at
the pond. It smelled terrific. It really did. I wished
I could have just sat there with my eyes closed and
my hands on my ears, just smelling that good pipe
smell. But no way! There was Sam's poster staring
right up at me from his desk like some ghost.

For about the eleven millionth time, I had to
explain that no, I wasn't trying to start some all-girl

army to fight boys and it was a consciousness-raising group and all that.

Mr. Baker said that a lot of parents were calling up, and they were pretty upset. He said the next time anyone wanted to put up a poster in school, they should bring it to the office first. He was going to send a memo to all the teachers, so that everyone would know and the school wouldn't get into mix-ups and misunderstandings and all that.

I know it sounds dumb, but I just forgot about Mr. Baker being a principal and everything. I told him about Miss Witherspoon and the phone number and her wanting to come to the meeting and how I was really worried that my father wouldn't get the Woodbury Central job because I didn't look to my English and how probably no one would want to be in the consciousness-raising group anyway with Miss Witherspoon bossing everyone around.

Before I knew it, I was feeling lousy. Down, down, down. Worse than the day before.

Mr. Baker just sat there and listened. What I really like about him is if you have a problem, he doesn't say "Think about the poor people in India" or "Ten thousand people just lost their homes in an earthquake in Peru," the way some grown-ups do. What they mean is that your problem isn't a real problem. That really gets me. But Mr. Baker, you could just tell he took your problems seriously. He just sat there puffing on his pipe before he said anything.

He said that he had known Miss Witherspoon for years and was still kind of scared of her. "But," he said, "even though she can be kind of sharp, she usually is pretty fair. When all is said and done, you can count on Abigail Witherspoon to tell the difference between apples and oranges."

He thought that she really wouldn't let my goofing up affect her decision about an architect for Woodbury Central.

As for wrecking the consciousness-raising group, he didn't know. "She might just surprise you," he said.

I felt like this Eskimo who had been walking across the hottest desert in Africa, all dressed for the North Pole. All of a sudden someone gives him a bathing suit and whammo! There he is swimming around in some oasis!

If Mr. Baker was right, Dad would *have* to get the Woodbury job. I mean, it just wasn't possible for anyone to design it better than Dad.

Sometimes talking to people is a funny thing. I mean nothing had really changed, but there I was—an Eskimo in an oasis. I kept thinking about that all the way back to Mrs. Martin's room.

9

WEDNESDAY AFTER-
noons are about the best time at our school. They
have something called release time. The kids who
go to church school for religious instruction leave
at two. Naturally they don't try and teach us anything after that.

You can get your homework done or mess
around in the art room if Mr. Dunlap, the art
teacher, is in a good mood. Sometimes he's really
fun and tells jokes and fools around and lets us do
all sorts of stuff. But sometimes it's "Don't touch
this" and "Don't touch that" and you can tell he
wishes you'd fall down some big hole and disap-
pear forever.

If you're a boy, you can go to the gym and play
basketball or something. But the best thing you can
do is to go to the library.

Mrs. Cavalari, the librarian, is this really nice
person. She's kind of always the same. I know that
she probably thinks a lot of the Dewey Decimal
System and the card catalog and all that stuff, but

what she mostly likes is books and people and getting them together.

She gave Suzy and me some books on Women's Lib and this neat book of poems called *Girls Can Too!* There was this poem in it about some kid whose best friend was named Suzy. She moved away and the kid in the poem felt all sad and rotten. I knew just how she felt. I mean, I'd die or something if my Suzy moved away.

We started to read the other books, but they were so long. They were interesting and all that, but it would have taken about five years to read them.

What we wanted to find were messages to put in the fortune cookies. "One of the reasons women earn less than men is that they are simply excluded from whole categories of work—the most lucrative ones." I mean, it's important to know something like that, but it doesn't exactly go right with fortune cookies.

Mrs. Cavalari let us use her paper cutter to cut strips of paper for the cookies. We just decided to try to think up our own messages to put on them, instead of trying to find really brilliant ones in a book.

Another thing about Mrs. Cavalari is she lets you talk quietly in the library. It's not like some church or anything.

Suzy and I started discussing what we would print on the messages. Holly and Julie came over to see what we were doing. They started thinking up things, too. By the time the bell rang for final dismissal, we had a bunch of messages. The only hitch was that we didn't have time to check the spelling. I am this really terrible speller. Maybe Miss Witherspoon was on a diet and wouldn't eat cookies anyway.

10

DID YOU EVER MAKE
fortune cookies? Maybe you don't even know what
they are. If you get to go to a Chinese restaurant,
you'll have them with dessert. They're these neat
little crunchy things with a message inside, a kind
of mysterious message.

The only bad thing about going to a Chinese
restaurant is that it makes you wish you were Chinese, so you could get to eat Chinese food all the
time! There's nothing to do about it if you're not.
The next best thing is to have a Chinese person for
your best friend. You can't have Suzy Suong because she's already MY best friend.

Suzy's grandmother, who is this really neat
person, had already made the batter by the time
we got home from school. I wish that I could speak
Chinese, mostly so that I could have a real conversation with Suzy's grandmother.

Anyhow, here's how you make fortune cookies, in case you want to try them yourself: First you
crack three eggs in a bowl and beat them like

crazy. When you think your arms will break off if
you have to beat them anymore, stop. Then throw
in a half-cup of brown sugar and a half-cup of flour,
the all-purpose kind. Get one of those half-teaspoon
measuring spoons and fill it with lemon extract.
(Don't bother tasting it. It's really horrible!) Just
empty it into the bowl with the other stuff. Then
beat the whole mess together, until it's thick and
gloppy. Get out a heavy skillet, and you're ready to
go!

Suzy and I took turns cooking them. Here's
how. You take a soup spoon. When you think the
griddle is hot, start plopping spoonfuls of batter on
it. Don't get carried away or anything. Three at a
time is enough!

Then take the tip of the spoon and spread the
blobs of batter into tiny pancakes, about three
inches wide. Flip them over when they're done on
one side. Cook the other side and shovel them on
to a platter. You might mess up a few, but if you
don't overdo it, you should have about thirty little
pancakes when you're through.

The tricky part is turning those pancakes into
fortune cookies. You have to hold a pancake between your thumb and your first two fingers. It
kind of makes a cup. Then slip the fortune into the
cup part. Press the edges of the pancake together
until it's sealed. If it absolutely won't seal, then
kind of glue it together with a little of the batter.

If you're one of those people who plans ahead,
good. If you keep them a while, your cookies will
be crispier and won't look as droopy as the ones

Suzy and I made. Planning ahead is just not my thing!

Suzy still had the box from her new sneakers. We lined it with wax paper and put the cookies in little rows. They really looked pretty good, like they came from the store or something.

"You know," Suzy said, "maybe we could go into the fortune cookie business, you and me. We could fix boxes of them and sell them. You could type the messages on your father's typewriter!"

Isn't that a great idea? That's what I mean about Suzy. She's always thinking up these great things to do. Oh Suzy! Don't *you* ever move away!

We were sitting in her bedroom talking when the phone rang. We almost always play in Suzy's room because she has these two little brothers that hang around if someone comes over to visit her. I kind of wish I had a little brother to boss around, but Suzy says it's not worth it.

Anyhow, guess who the phone was for. Me! It was David. David hardly talks to me at home anymore. Why was he calling me at Suzy's?

"When are you coming home?" he asked.

I had been kind of hoping Suzy's mother would get home from work and invite me for supper. I just said I didn't know.

"Well, you better hurry up," David said. He wouldn't say why or anything. I didn't feel much like going. What makes him think he can tell me what to do? On the other hand, it must be something kind of important. I mean, David never called me up like that before.

11

THE SECOND I OPENED the door, I knew something was strange. I stood still a minute, trying to sniff out what was different. The house was filled with the smell of baking bread. Mom bakes bread every once in a while, so I knew that wasn't it. Then all of a sudden I realized that it wasn't something you could smell. It was music, David's kind of music, blasting right in the living room. Usually he listens to it closed in his room like he's at some hotel or something. But not this time!

Then I saw why. There was this girl in the house. She had this long brown hair, the shiny, bouncy kind they have on T.V. You know the kind of hair I mean. Sometimes there's this girl crying on the beach because she uses the wrong toothpaste or else she's talking to her boyfriend on the telephone and he has v.d. or her mother is so young-looking because she takes Geritol. It doesn't really matter what they're saying because all you think about is how terrific the girl's hair looks. I'm sure you know the exact type. But what was a girl like that doing with a creep like David?

David actually got up when I came in! You have to know David to realize what a miracle that is. He walked across the room and touched my arm. His hand felt like ice cubes, if you can imagine what sweaty ice cubes feel like.

"Well, this is her," he said to Bouncylocks. "Dorothy, meet Meg."

He seemed to be trying to say something to me with his eyes, but I couldn't figure out what.

I had to bite hard on my lower lip to keep from saying something like "Are you the Dorothy in David's poems?"

She said "Hi," and I said "Hi." Then she asked David to turn down the music because she wanted to talk to me. ME! Can you imagine that??

She started talking to me about the consciousness-raising group. It turned out she was a Women's Libber, too. She said a lot of junk about how glad she was to know David so that she could get to know me and how all women are sisters, did I know that, and would I mind if she started her very own consciousness-raising group at the high school. Blah, blah, blah! I'm out of breath just trying to tell you half of the stuff she said!

Before I even got a chance to say that for creep's sake I didn't own all of Women's Lib or anything, David said, "Can I join your group, Dorothy?"

He just sort of blurted it out. Then his face got all red. Instant sunburn.

"Oh, David," she said, "you're wonderful."
She really laid it on thick about how sensitive he
was and how great it would be if he did join her
group.

David just sat there with his red face and his
arms and legs hanging all over the place. He
lapped up every word she said. It was so disgust-
ing I almost puked.

Just then Mom came in. I didn't think I could
stand one more minute of that phony girl and
David. But Mom just wasn't with it!

"I hope you'll stay for supper, Dorothy," she
said.

I wished old Dorothy would say that her uncle
had just arrived from Afghanistan and she couldn't,
but no luck.

"I'd just love to stay, if it's O.K. with my
folks," she said.

She called home and naturally she could stay.
Then she got real busy helping Mom with supper,
which is what I usually do. Old David even got
into the act setting the table. I'm not terribly clean
or anything, but yuk! I just don't like the idea of
David touching my plate and silverware and all
that stuff before I use it.

Anyhow, it was pretty obvious no one needed
me. I went to my room and started my math homework. Hanging around those two would spoil anyone's appetite.

But supper went better than I thought it
would. Dad was very excited about a new house he
was designing. It was going to be on a real steep

slope, kind of a cliff. Dad talked about how the house would just hang there, and I could almost see it.

I almost always like my father an enormous bunch, but when he's all psyched up about something like with the cliff house, I love him extra. His eyes get this very special way, and I don't even mind that he teases me sometimes.

You could tell that Dorothy was really listening to Dad, which was kind of amazing. I thought that all she knew how to do was talk and kind of swish all that hair around.

After supper Dorothy said she and David would clean up the dishes. It was kind of like a miracle because old David didn't even complain.

Mom decided to go with me to walk Sin. She even talked Dad into coming along. I thought that wasn't very good manners even if Dorothy was a big talker.

It was a beautiful night with millions of stars. You could just tell Sin really was enjoying it. He kept perking up his ears, listening for something I couldn't hear.

He's a funny dog. He sniffs and sniffs before he decides to lift his leg, like he's giving some special leaf or patch of grass the Good Housekeeping Seal of Approval.

I wonder if he approves of Dorothy. It's really a pity that dogs can't talk. I mean, Sin probably has some very intelligent thoughts.

We were way ahead of Mom and Dad. When I started back they were just standing at the edge of the fields. Just standing with their arms around each other in the night. Together they made a kind of whole thing, a kind of majority. A majority of two. Does that make any sense to you?· What I mean is there was just the two of them without David and me, but they didn't look like they were missing any parts. I guess I just never thought of them as separate—without us—a family themselves.

I wonder if David and Dorothy will get to be like that someday, and what about me?

I let Sin off his leash, and we started running. Half chasing each other. Going in circles. I held my arms out stiff like airplane wings and started twirling and zooming across the fields. I felt better than O.K. I felt terrific! I was a majority, too. A majority of one, zooming through the night. Me, Meg Prescott, and her faithful servant, My Sin.

12

DAVID LEFT A NOTE saying he was walking you-know-who home. Isn't that ridiculous? Was she some little kid who might get lost or was she afraid of the dark?

Every time I started thinking about THE MEETING, I got all butterflies and goose bumps.

My father has this way of figuring things, kind of a philosophy. He always says you should do what you can about something, and when there's nothing more you can do, stop worrying. I guess there wasn't any more I could do about the meeting, but it wasn't so easy to stop worrying about it. I tried to keep busy doing my homework. I even brushed my hair and took a shower, but old Abigail Witherspoon kept pushing herself into everything I tried to do.

I was sitting in bed, trying to get interested in this terrible mystery story, the kind you can figure out from the first page. David came glumping into my room.

"Here," he said and threw me this big pack of

bubble gum. He left before I could say "Thanks" or anything.

I could hear him mooching around in his room, kind of singing. The funny thing was that he left his door open. He almost never does that.

When I was this real little kid, maybe four or five years old, things used to wake me up in the night. You know, like thunderstorms or a bad dream. I'd just go right into David's room and climb into bed with him. He'd talk to me until I stopped being scared or I fell asleep or something. That was so long ago, but I'll never forget how I used to be able to tell him everything, even dumb little kid stuff, and he could make it better.

I was wishing that things could be like that again when David just walked into my room and slumped into my chair. It's a rocking chair. David kind of hung out all over it. It isn't that he's fat or anything. It's just that he's got an awful lot of arms and legs.

"What's new?" he asked, like he hadn't seen me in six months.

I never know what to say when anyone asks me that. It seems like you have this real boring life if you just say "nothing." I was so amazed that David was even talking to me, I couldn't even say "What's new with *you?*"

David was trying to rock and kept bumping the chair into the wall. I didn't want to tell him he was sitting on my clothes for the next day.

"Well, what do you think of her?" he asked.

43

"You mean Abigail Witherspoon?" I said.

"No, dumbhead. Dorothy. What do you think of Dorothy?"

I almost told him what I really thought about old blah-blah mouth, who couldn't even walk home by herself. But something about the way David looked made me stop.

"Well, she's a real good talker," I said. "Her hair is nifty, really beautiful."

"Yeah. You're right. She really is wonderful." That's what old David says, sitting there on my clothes with this dumb smile on his face, banging the rocker into the wall.

Creeps! I never said she was wonderful!

Then David said, "You know, Meg, it's a good thing that you're having all those drippy little kids come over. It was wrong of me to hassle you about it."

I just sat there and watched the mark on the wall get bigger.

"Take a girl like Dorothy. She never was conscious when she was a little kid. She had to take old home economics instead of wood shop or metal shop, just because she was unconscious."

I got this picture of Dorothy, walking around in the high school like some sleepwalker. Actually David didn't look so wide-awake himself.

"I've got to go now," David said.

But actually he didn't go. He just sat there.

"Want your light off?"

"Yes, thanks," I told him.

All of a sudden it was much easier to stop thinking about Miss Witherspoon. Now I had David to figure out. I kept thinking of the high school with the halls full of kids. The boys were rushing down the halls, opening lockers, gabbing with each other, going places. But the girls, all of the girls, were walking down the halls half-asleep, with their long hair all brushed and shiny.

13

THE DAY OF THE MEET-
ing I just muddled through school. I rushed home
as soon as I could to get there before any other kids
did. When I dashed into the kitchen to touch base
with Mom, who do you think was drinking tea with
her?

Wow! I'd seen Miss Witherspoon's picture in
the paper and talked to her on the phone, but that
hadn't made me ready for the real thing in living
color!

It's not that Miss Witherspoon has about five
million wrinkles on her face or that she always
looks like she's on her way to a rummage sale to
donate her hat. It's the way she gets it all together.
Like you shake hands with a skinny old lady who
wears white gloves. Crunch! It feels like you've
just met your favorite football player. I mean
you'll just have to meet her yourself to really understand what I'm talking about.

Anyhow, she said that she was getting to know
my mother and was looking forward to getting to

know me. I guess I said "Thank you," but before I could say any other dumb thing the doorbell started ringing. I just told everyone to throw their coats across my bed. Before long there was a mountain of coats. I wished that I could crawl under them and hibernate like a bear until the whole world was liberated!

Kids were sitting all over the living room floor. Samantha Mahan had come, after all, but she still wasn't speaking to me. At the back of the room I saw Miss Witherspoon sitting on a kitchen chair, still holding her teacup.

Suzy brought the fortune cookies. The two of us had talked about how to start things. But talking is one thing and doing is something else! She shot me her special don't-goof-up-now look.

I raised my arm the way we had agreed I should and said who I was and asked everyone to take turns saying who they were. I guess I did it all right except my voice came out too loud, and I forgot to make a fist the way Suzy said I should.

One by one each girl got up and said her name, but I nearly dropped my teeth when Miss Witherspoon got up just like one of the kids and said, "I'm Abby."

You could tell most of the kids hadn't even noticed her in the back of the room. I know just how they felt. It's not exactly relaxing to be in the same room with someone who looks like a great-grandmother and a teacher rolled into one.

"Traitor!" Sam hissed under her breath.

All the bad vibrations shook me up and instead of passing around the fortune cookies like we planned, I started this big defense of Miss Witherspoon like a lawyer or something. I said how she was a Women's Libber before there even was Women's Lib and how lucky we were to have her come to our meeting and did she have any advice. She did!

"First, please call me Abby," said Miss Witherspoon.

That was going to be as natural as calling the Queen of England Lizzy.

Then she said, "Don't ever let anyone tell you that you can't do something because you're girls. The only thing a girl can't be is a father!"

She said something about how different the world is now than when she was a kid and how we have different problems than she did and that we should just do our own thing. "Proceed as if I were not here." That's what she said!

It had gotten very quiet in the room while Miss Witherspoon was speaking. Suzy passed out the fortune cookies. Luckily Miss Witherspoon, I mean Abby, didn't take one. Maybe she had false teeth or something, but at least I could stop worrying about my spelling.

There's no use pretending that I'm some kind of expert about consciousness-raising or that I'm some born leader like Joan of Arc. I said if anybody had anything to say they should say it and that maybe the messages in the fortune cookies would help them think of stuff.

Suzy is kind of a poet, and she made some of

the messages rhyme. One said, "It's cause boys get to use the gym, She wishes she was born a HIM!" Naturally it had to be Sam Mahan who got that one. It doesn't take much to make Sam fighting mad. Being reminded that the boys got to use the gym after lunch every day and during release time made her furious.

One of the girls from St. Mary's said that at their school it was all girls. Nobody got to use the gym anyhow except during classes, so what was Sam so mad about.

Julie said the real trouble was grown-ups. They just don't realize that girls like to do sports as much as boys. That got Sam going again about Little League and football and all the sports girls got left out of.

From the back of the room a lemonade voice said, "It seems to me that if a group of girls present a petition to their principal, a more democratic program for use of the gymnasium could be made."

Every time A.W. spoke it seemed to freeze everybody for a few seconds. Once they started to thaw out again, most of the kids seemed to think a petition would be a good way to start.

But Sam said, "O.K., Abby. But what about Little League?"

Poor Sam. Little League is an obsession of hers. It's something that really keeps bothering her. She's a terrific baseball player, but every year when she tries to sign up for Little League it's "No girls allowed." They keep asking her why she doesn't start an all-girls softball league, but Sam wants to play baseball. And she wants to play it with the boys!

Nobody had any really good suggestions about what Sam could do. Jane Pixley said the big problem was much more than Little League. She had the fortune cookie that said "What are little girls made of?" That was the one Mom gave me the idea for.

"I've been thinking and thinking," said Jane. "Nobody really stops to think about what girls are made of, especially the grown-ups who make all the dumb rules. What we have to do is something big. Something that will show them girls are more than sugar and spice!"

14

JANE PIXLEY WILL PROB-
ably be the first lady president of the United States.
She can really get people excited.

"What should we show them girls are made
of? How should we show them?" Jane can really
sound like some senator or somebody.

"We should show them girls are made of mus-
cle," said Sam.

"And brains!" said Suzy.

Sam wanted to have a big tug-of-war, girls
against boys, in front of Town Hall where they
have the football rallies.

Suzy thought that was too chancy. What if the
boys won? She wanted to have a debate.

Everybody started arguing about which would
be a better thing to do, and then Julie dropped the
bomb. She said what the real Women's Libbers did
was burn their bras.

I really wish they had never done that. Just
say "Women's Lib" to some of the dumb people

around this town and all they can say is something stupid about bra burners.

But Julie really thinks the bra burners were right. She said they really showed that all women didn't want to go through life doing things like shaving their legs just so they could be in some old beauty contest. She seemed to be convincing a lot of kids that's what we should do.

I was kind of dying, when good old Sam shook them up. She wanted to know how we could burn our bras when most of us didn't even own one.

Then one kid said we could take one of our mother's, but somebody else said that was like cheating. Another person thought we should burn our undershirts, but nobody could figure out what that would prove. We kicked around one idea after another, and I was sure we wouldn't end up doing anything.

Just then Miss Witherspoon said, "Taffy Teen Dolls. Why don't we burn Taffy Teen Dolls?"

It was such a neat idea, so perfect, that nobody said anything. It took a few seconds for the meaning to sink in. Then Sam yelled, "Right on, Abby!"

There was a buzz of "Yeah," "Great," and "Brilliant." But I suddenly was aware of silence. The kind that is so heavy you can hear it.

Monica Scalise was sitting right next to me. All the time we had been talking, she had been busy changing her Taffy Teen Doll into different outfits. Just then Taffy was wearing her yellow bikini, all ready for a day at the beach with her boyfriend Jeff. For the first time Monica stopped fooling around with Taffy. She just sat there with this funny expression on her face. Quietly she put old Taffy into this special suitcase and mumbled something about having to be home by five.

Some of the other kids had to go home, too, so we decided that we'd all get together at Julie's house in a week. Taffy would burn the following Saturday, and we needed to get a lot of details straight.

Finally the last kid picked up the last coat from my bed. I climbed right in the middle and started to kind of jump and bounce up and down. The meeting was over, over, over! It had turned out a million times better than I ever even hoped! Abby Witherspoon had turned out to be the very best part of it! Burn, Taffy, burn!

15

IT'S FUNNY THE WAY
time goes. Do you ever think about it? Like sometimes a day lasts five hundred years. Other times it
seems like only three hours and fifteen minutes
have gone by and there you are—back in your pajamas, cleaning your teeth and saying "Goodnight"
again.

It's probably a good thing that one of the very
first things you get taught is that there are twenty-
four hours in a day and seven days in a week. If
they left it up to me, I'd have all the days different
amounts. Some of the weeks would have fifty days.
Anyhow, the week after our meeting seemed to
just whiz by—a three–and–a–half dayer.

Mrs. Gonzalez, she's kind of Mom's favorite
patient, had twins. The babies were O.K., but Mrs.
Gonzalez had "complications." Mom was staying
late at the hospital an awful lot, and we got to eat
pizza from Roma Di Notte three times. I kind of
wanted to tell Mom about the Taffy Teen Doll
business, but we just didn't get much time alone.

Also I didn't want Dorothy to blab it all over the high school until the right time.

I guess I really should tell you this. Dorothy is always hanging around our house these days. I don't know how she and David can stand each other. I mean she is such a blah-blah talker and he is such a slob. Or anyhow he was such a slob. You'll never believe this, but ever since Dorothy, David has gotten like Mr. Clean. He takes showers every day, even when he doesn't smell. He uses dental floss, which is kind of weird considering he hardly ever brushes his teeth.

At school all we talked about during lunch period was Taffy Teen Dolls. The kids that buy hot lunch can't sit at the same table with the kids that bring lunch, the "brown baggers." I noticed that Monica Scalise started buying hers.

Almost everybody had a Taffy Teen Doll, whether they really still played with them or not. Julie really hated to burn hers. So did Suzy. Those two are so practical, especially Suzy. Suzy kind of thought maybe we should just have this Taffy Teen Doll sale and use the money to hire a lawyer or something. But Jane and Sam, they kept everyone's head straight about just why we had to BURN Taffy. Sam started thinking that Taffy was a bigger enemy than boys!

I had never even thought about Taffy Teen Dolls meaning anything. Aunt Francie gave me one for my birthday. I just kind of left it on my dresser until tadpole season. When I needed the space for all my tadpole stuff, I put Taffy in the closet somewhere and never thought about her again. I mean Taffy wasn't like my old beat-up doll I had when I was real little. You could cuddle up with that doll. Who'd want to cuddle up with Taffy? A computer probably.

A lot of girls are really into the whole Taffy Teen business. All their money goes into buying new clothes for her. Not so much this year, but last year it seemed that almost every kid I knew wanted new junk for Taffy for Christmas, instead of skis or ice skates.

All those lunch hour rap sessions really got us thinking. I mean Taffy is kind of a big trap. She's this glamour girl, always dressed up. She's got a perfect figure and beauty-parlor hair. All she does is change her clothes and stand around looking pretty for her boyfriend Jeff.

Can you imagine Taffy going on a hike or painting the porch or getting all messed up washing the car? I'll bet she doesn't even play touch football with Jeff. Do you think Taffy would ever read a book and really think about it? Like when Suzy and I read *Charlotte's Web*, we cried so hard and ached inside. Old Taffy would have to worry about her eye makeup.

Jane said the sneaky part of Taffy is that she gets people kind of wanting to be like her. Julie said that anyone would have to be crazy to want to be like a doll. But Jane reminded her how the two of them had started doing chest exercises during the summer. Wasn't that so they could be like Taffy? Wasn't it?

What really surprises me is none of the kids really minded Miss Witherspoon. They all thought she was pretty much O.K. from the beginning. Sam was the only one who called her Abby, but we all made a pact to try. After all, that was what she wanted, wasn't it?

I began to feel all right about Miss Witherspoon, too. She isn't the crab I thought she was. She certainly wouldn't be the one to jinx Dad's plan for the new school. In fact, I thought she might like it a little extra. After all, we're in the same club, kind of.

16

JUST MENTION THAT
somebody is getting a divorce to my Aunt Francie.
Just mention it, and you'd think the world was
coming to an end.

"The poor children! What a tragedy for the
children!" That's pretty much what Aunt Francie
always says. She probably doesn't know any kids
whose folks are divorced or she wouldn't say that.

Some divorced kids really have it made. Suzy
says it's a racket the way they get doubles of good
stuff like on Christmas and birthdays. Since my
friend Michael's parents got their divorce, he gets
to stay with his father in New York City every
other weekend. They do really neat things like riding their bikes in Central Park and going to the
circus and exploring all the secret places in the
city.

The best part of getting your parents divorced
is that you aren't in the middle of arguments and
bad vibrations. Aunt Francie, she never thinks
about all the kids whose mothers and fathers don't

like each other. She should just spend an overnight with some of the kids I know!

The best deal is when your parents get married to other people. Do you know why? I have it figured out this way. Cinderella and Hansel and Gretel, all those "once upon a time" characters, have really given stepparents such lousy reputations that I think most of them do backflips to be extra nice.

Anyhow, my theory kind of explains why the refreshments were so good at Julie's house, which is where we were having the second meeting. Julie's stepmother put out a big platter of doughnuts—two kinds—and apple cider. Being able to have seconds kept us from being too disappointed that there were a lot less kids. Besides, Abby said it was normal for curiosity seekers to go to first meetings. She said what we need is quality, not quantity.

Right off the bat, we had to decide what to call ourselves. Sam thought The Avengers sounded good, but Jane Pixley nixed that fast. She said we needed a "positive image" so Hell's Angels wouldn't do either. Holly said we should call ourselves the Circleville Campfire Girls because, after all, we were having a fire. Don't you think that's kind of sneaky? Then Suzy said why not call ourselves the Saturday Sisters because Saturday was the day we were going to shake things up. We all liked that, especially the way the "S's" slurped together.

We really had a lot of work to do. Do you know

what a manifesto is? It's kind of like the Declaration of Independence. If you're doing something—something important—and it really matters that people understand, you should have a manifesto. Jane and Holly started to write ours. We had been talking about the whole Taffy Teen business all week long. Sometimes things that sound O.K. between bites of your peanut butter and jelly sandwich don't look right when you write them down. I mean a manifesto is something kids just like us might end up studying in school in a hundred years. You can't just write down any old thing.

Let's face it. Adults think of a bunch of stuff you wouldn't. Like publicity. I got the job of calling the newspaper and asking them to send a photographer to come to Town Hall at 10:00 on Saturday and writing a release for the radio station that told what was happening. We wouldn't be accomplishing much if we burned Taffy Teen and no one got to know why. Sam was working on posters and Suzy was making signs to hold.

The thing of it was that I don't think any of us thought about how important publicity was except Abby. We were all mostly worried that between all of us we only had nine Taffy Teen Dolls. We didn't think they'd look like much. Jane said we should have fifty. Otherwise she thought we'd look like real goof-ups.

Abby was the one who convinced us we had enough dolls. She said even less would do. What was important was not how many kids wanted to burn their Taffy Teen Dolls, but why. It's funny

MANIFESTO OF THE SATURDAY SISTERS

WHEREAS most grown-ups don't even wonder
why they do things the way they do
and WHEREAS the way things get done girls get
treated as if they'd break or they're stupid
and WHEREAS boys get to play on the team,
while girls only get to be the cheerleaders
and WHEREAS boys get to build things *that last*
in shop, while girls cook oatmeal in Home Ec.
and WHEREAS boys grow up to be the airplane
pilots, while girls get to be the airplane
waitresses
and WHEREAS boys grow up to be the bosses
and girls grow up to say, "Yes, boss"
and WHEREAS from the time they're kids to the
time they're grown up, female creatures get
labeled
and WHEREAS that label means female creatures can't or shouldn't or couldn't possibly do
a whole bunch of things

WE DEMAND AN END TO LABELS!

WE PROCLAIM GIRLS TO BE HUMAN
BEINGS, NOT DECORATIONS!

THE SATURDAY SISTERS WILL NOT
SLEEP UNTIL ALL SISTERS WAKE UP!

because right then and there we might have decided to wait a few months or call the whole thing off. But we didn't.

We started batting around the Manifesto that Jane and Holly read. Everybody stuck in something and it really ended up sounding pretty great, which is why I'm sticking in a copy for you.

17

WELL, ONE GOOD THING you can say about Taffy Teen Dolls is that they don't burn! At least, you might say it's a good thing if you don't happen to be holding a sign that says WHY TAFFY MUST BURN or one that says WE KINDLE A NEW FLAME. It probably helps you appreciate how safe Taffy Teen is if you're not holding a big pail of water like Suzy. It even helps more if you're not the person who called up *The Evening Record* so that the whole disaster can get in the paper.

Things started out fine. There weren't too many people around Town Hall. Some ladies from the Garden Club were collecting pine cones in big plastic bags to decorate for Christmas. A bunch of kids were riding their bikes around the parking lot.

Mr. Tonioli, the town police chief and police force rolled into one, was just sitting in his car. I think he was dreaming of the great bank robbery that someone might pull off at County Savings and he'd get to corner the crooks. He always makes me think of a crocodile half dozing in the river, waiting for a catch.

There were some people who had come especially to see us. Mrs. Cavalari, the school librarian, was there with some real little kid. Dorothy and a few girls from high school were there. They held a sign that said RIGHT ON LITTLE SISTERS. That really was kind of nice. Don't you think?

Sam played "Taps" on her trumpet to start things officially like for a real ceremony. Everyone thought Sam should play "Reveille," but she kind of mucked up the notes, so we settled for "Taps."

Actually, old politician Jane Pixley turned the fact that it's easier to play "Taps" into something good. That kid is too much! Before she read the Manifesto, she said something about "Taps" marking the end of an age when boys had more rights than girls. I'm sure that's almost exactly what she said. It takes a special kind of guts to say that with a straight face. Don't you think so?

Anyhow, by the time Jane finished reading the Manifesto, quite a little crowd had gathered. The Garden Club ladies and the bicycle kids had decided to check us out. The policeman, Mr. Tonioli, had gotten out of his car. He was leaning against it and looking very thoughtful.

We were planning to burn the Taffy Teen Dolls in the exact place where they have the bonfire before the football games. There's kind of a circle of big stones. You know, like at a campfire.

Julie's sister who got to be in all the high school plays and was going to go to honest-to-goodness drama school and be a live actress had kind of sat in at our planning meeting. She had these ideas of how we could give things "dramatic impact." A "musical overture" which turned out to be Sam blowing her trumpet was her idea. She thought up that each kid should put her Taffy Teen Doll on the fire one by one. She wanted us all to wear sheets draped like Roman senators or Greeks. She wasn't sure which. As each kid placed Taffy on the "funeral pyre," she was supposed to say, "I commend this worthless body to the flames because blah, blah, blah."

None of us would go along with the sheet business. It was just too silly. I mean I can be as phony as the next guy, but nobody wants to be that phony! What we did decide to do was have each kid put her doll on the pile and say, "I'm burning Taffy Teen because . . ." Then she was supposed to give her own reason. After everyone had done that, Miss Witherspoon was going to light the fire. You know how some parents are about kids using matches. Besides, Abby didn't have a Taffy Teen Doll. It only seemed right to give her the honor. She really thought the whole thing up.

Everything went fine up to then. "I'm burning Taffy because she's not like a real person," Julie said.

"I'm burning Taffy because she's a phony," said Holly.

"I'm burning Taffy because all she ever thinks about is clothes, clothes, clothes. If you do that, you'll never get to be a detective or anything else good," said Suzy.

But Sam. Leave it to Sam. She was the last person to put her doll on the pile. It was still in the plastic box. Brand-new. Sam kind of set the scene.

"I'm burning Taffy because she stinks." That's what Sam said.

We found out. She sure does!

18

ABBY WAS WEARING A hat that you could tell was a special-occasion one. The feather on it curled like a question mark when she bent over the pile of Taffy Teen Dolls and struck a match. It was an extra long one like they use for fireplaces.

I don't know why, but it didn't hit me. I just watched that long match burn down and go out. I didn't realize that it hadn't started a fire.

There was something about all those Taffys in their jumpsuits and mini-skirts and bikinis that was making me feel kind of flaky. To tell you the truth, I still feel flaky just thinking about them.

Did you ever see one of those science fiction programs on T.V.? These real guys are just cruising around in their spaceship, when whammo! There they are in another time zone or on some strange planet of look-alike people. All those Taffys. They were look-alike plastic people.

Maybe I didn't tell you I did this social studies project on the Salem witch trials. Somehow my feelings about Taffy got all mixed up with those people who got burned at the stake. Anyhow, I was beginning to feel like some kind of a rat. Those Taffys looked so real. I was forgetting how unreal they really are.

It was Suzy groaning "Oh no!" that brought me back to reality.

Abby had just struck the fourth match, and something was happening. Taffy's ball gown was burning! Hey, her beach pajamas caught fire! But before the match had even burned down, the clothes stopped burning.

Abby touched the match to those shiny blond heads. The make-believe hair kind of melted away. It didn't even flame up!

Jane tore up the piece of cardboard the Manifesto was printed on, and Abby lighted that. Everyone gave a big sigh of relief. At least the cardboard burned!

But oh, Sam Mahan! You called it right. Did Taffy ever stink! It was as though some mad scientist had smashed all the test tubes in his laboratory. You could smell all the potions! Yuk! My stomach is still going flip-flop.

Anyhow, no sooner had the cardboard started to burn than Chief Tonioli ambled over.

"Misdemeanor. You're committing a misdemeanor, Ma'am. You're not allowed to burn things in this town without a permit. We got a dump, you know. You want to burn something, bring it down there." That's pretty much what the chief said to Miss Witherspoon.

I didn't know what got into Miss Witherspoon. I mean Abby. Whether it was getting the full blast of all those chemicals or what.

Without answering the chief, she took the big pot of water from Suzy. We all thought she was going to toss it on the fire, which wasn't really a fire. It was a smolder. Just smoke and smells. But then she turned. Very carefully she tossed the water right into Chief Tonioli's face.

"Right on, Abby!" shouted Sam. "That's the way!"

The rest of us were too amazed to say or do anything. That includes Ms. Jane Pixley! I mean, what would you have done? We hadn't practiced how to go limp or anything.

The kids on the bikes gawked. The Garden Club ladies were "goodness graciousing." Really, I wish you had been there.

Chief Tonioli stood still and glowered at Abby, while the water went drip, drip, drip off the tip of his nose. Abby stared back at him. The feather in her hat became an exclamation point.

"Setting a fire without a permit, that's a misdemeanor," said Chief Tonioli. "But attacking a police officer, that's a felony. I could arrest you for that."

The chief's face was sunburn red. Even his neck was red.

Abby looked straight at him, cool as can be. But Sam said something like "Just you try it." That was all the chief needed.

"All right," he said. "You're under arrest!"

Before any of us could think of what to do or how to do it, the chief was advising Miss Witherspoon of her rights and telling her how there'd be a hearing within three days and a whole bunch of other stuff. He was taking her into Town Hall for fingerprinting! Abigail Witherspoon in jail!

"Don't worry, Abby. We'll spring you!" Sam shouted.

Abby looked at us very quietly. A kind of smile spread across her face, if you can imagine it. I could swear she winked at me like we had some conspiracy going.

19

THIS WAS ONE TIME that I was not going to depend on Suzy Suong, Private Eye, to deal with the long arm of the law. I got home as fast as I could. Luckily both my parents were there. The three of us were back at Town Hall before you could say Abigail Witherspoon.

The newspaper reporter was asking the girls in our gang questions and writing down what each of us was saying. He had us pose around the fire and took pictures of the signs. I remembered how bored he had been by the whole business! I saw him yawning while Jane was reading the Manifesto. But now it was a different ball game. He wanted to know what the Manifesto said word for word. Luckily Jane had a copy folded up in her pocket. She made him copy it on the spot and give it right back to her.

Mom and Dad went right into Town Hall. In case you ever need to find the police station in this

20

ALL DURING SUPPER I
this picture of Abby stuck in my head. I
just see her crouched in her cell, holding a
of stale bread and sipping water from a tin
She was wearing a striped suit like you have
prison and a little round prison hat—but with
ther in it. Even if we weren't having Saturday
wreck, which is what David calls Mom's
ep-the-kitchen casseroles, I couldn't have
en much. Not with that picture of Abby in my
d.

We were all kind of quiet during supper.
aybe we were just talked out. All afternoon peo-
e had been calling. My friends' parents called to
lk with my parents. The radio station called to
k me a bunch of questions. Dorothy called. She
ad to have a whole conversation with Mom and
David and me. Jibber-jabber. Yak-yak. Ugh!

Just when we smelled the rolls burning, the
phone rang again. We all kind of groaned.

Guess who it was! It was the president of the

town, go downstairs. It's right past the tax office
before you get to "Men's."

Mom and Dad said the chief seemed kind of
relieved to see them. There isn't much of a jail in
our town. There's only this one section of the big
police room that's kind of caged in. The chief
hadn't put anyone in jail for so long that he was
having difficulty finding the key. He asked my
folks to guard the prisoner while he plowed
through his desk drawers.

Naturally my parents wanted to get Abby out
of there right away. The way they tell it, Miss
Witherspoon just thanked them very much for coming. "No," she didn't want a lawyer. "No," she
didn't want to be bailed out. The way she understood it she would have a hearing on Tuesday, and
"yes," that suited her fine.

Finally Chief Tonioli gave up on finding the
keys. It must have dawned on him that the lady he
had arrested was no plain old crackpot. He was beginning to feel sheepish about the whole thing.
He even asked Abby if maybe she was just playing a good-natured joke. Maybe they should just
forget about the arrest and the fingerprints and the
whole bit.

But Abby was determined to go the whole
route. She told the chief she was arrested and intended to stay arrested. Chief Tonioli didn't really
have any choice. Since she wasn't going to get herself bailed out or anything, and he couldn't find the
keys to the town jail anyhow, he had to put handcuffs on her and drive her to the county jail!

The reporter from *The Evening Record* and Lisa Davidson, the editor of the high school paper, were on their way into Town Hall, when Abby, the chief, and my parents came piling through the doors. Honestly, it was almost like on T.V., except there should have been more reporters. But Lisa and that guy from the *Record* acted like big city pros! It's a shame they didn't have tape recorders and microphones and stuff, but they asked the same kind of questions the big shot reporters ask.

"Yes," she was going to plead guilty. She used bigger words and better English when she said it, but what she meant was Chief Tonioli was a symbol of a whole system that she was throwing water at. Maybe it was wrong to burn Taffy Teen Dolls without a permit, but who gave schools and the whole of everything a permit to squoosh girls? She went on and on, almost listing the ways girls got the short end of the stick. Her voice was different than before. It was slow and steady, the way Mrs. Martin gives a vocabulary test. "Ardently. He cheered the team ARDENTLY." The reporters were writing down every word she said.

I felt so mixed up. Jail was about the worst thing that could happen to anyone. But Miss Witherspoon, I mean Abby, looked happier than I had ever seen her. I couldn't believe she could look that happy. I mean, she held up her hands with the handcuffs right on them and made the V for victory sign! For a while I thought she had gone absolutely batty.

Dad seemed to read my mind. He put his arm

around my shoulde
about Miss Withersp
what she was doing.
eye that he was pretty

I guess you think
took me all that time t
ing: Abigail Witherspo
for girls like it has neve
I mean, everybody in th
Sunday paper. If Abigail
jail, you can just bet eve
about why.

While Abby was climb
car, Jane started to cheer.
loud as we could: "Two, fo
we appreciate?"

I mean Abby really was
was really going to score for
only problem was where wer
decided that? Who was makin

Aunt Francie says if the W
get what they want they'll be s
Francie! I hope you're wrong.

school board. He must have been just about the only person in town who hadn't heard about Miss Witherspoon. He had just gotten back from playing golf. From where I was sitting, I could see Dad smiling his company manners smile and asking those automatic questions adults ask each other.

Then Dad's expression changed. You know how these phony novelists are always saying, "Her face dropped when she saw the butler had become a werewolf"? Well, honestly, that's just what happened to my father's face. Maybe it didn't drop, but it sure drooped. He was saying, "I see" and "Thanks for letting me know." I couldn't figure out what was happening until Dad told us.

When he did tell us, I couldn't believe what he was saying. I mean how could she? The whole school board—well, just about the whole school board—had pretty much decided that Dad's plan for Woodbury Central was the best. But Abigail Witherspoon, rat-fink Benedict Arnold Witherspoon, had some "serious reservations." She questioned if an independent architect like Dad could handle a big project like building a school. I can just hear her lemonade voice icing up Dad's chances with the school board! She thought Dad's plan was better, "more imaginative," but wouldn't Calvert, Koch and Prendergast be better able to give "architectural supervision"? I mean who ran over to Town Hall to get her out of jail? If Calvert, Koch and Prendergast were such on-top-of-it guys, one of them could have at least showed up!

When Mom told Dad to remember Miss Witherspoon didn't actually have a vote, he told her to stop being Mary Poppins. Everything anybody wanted to say turned out to be the wrong thing. We just kind of all sat there, shuffling Saturday Shipwreck around on our plates.

I really jumped at the chance to escape when Julie called and asked if I could sleep over at her house. Mom and Dad said I could go and remember my manners and don't forget my toothbrush and get to bed at a reasonable hour. I disappeared with my sleeping bag before they could change their minds.

21

BY THE TIME I GOT
to Julie's, Jane and Sam were there, and Suzy and
Holly were on the way. See what I mean about
stepmothers? All Julie probably said was, "Can I
have a friend sleep over?"

"Have them all over. Have a slumber party!"
That's what Julie's stepmother probably said.

We were all kind of excited to find ourselves
together in the middle of a party. Sometimes if you
have a few weeks to think about a party, when it finally comes off it's a drag. I mean you get thinking, wow, a party! It's going to be great! Then it
turns out to be some kid's parents are trying to
make you act like it's the nineteenth century and
you have to play dumb party games instead of
plain old games you like and you start having trouble talking to the same old kids you horsed around
with yesterday.

Julie's party wasn't a bit like that. The moon
was making it bright like day. Her folks said

"sure," we could fool around outside. "Just stay in the neighborhood."

First we played tag. When we got tired of doing that, Suzy said we should be gathering clues to help defend Abby. None of us really believed that Abby needed us to "prepare the case," as Suzy said. It just fit in with our wacky mood to pretend we were detectives. We hid behind trees and pretended all station wagons were suspicious vehicles. We turned up our collars and called each other numbers like Agent 007. Except I was being a double agent. Abigail Witherspoon could get forty years at hard labor for all I cared!

Then Suzy got the idea that we should really go collect the Taffy Teen Dolls because they were honest-to-goodness evidence. Since we knew they wouldn't burn, Jane thought it was really gross to just leave them in the bonfire pit.

Jane is really freaky about the environment. Do you know what she wants? She wants them to give the death penalty for littering, second offense. Jane says the death penalty would stop littering right away.

It could start with ten-year-olds because any kid that big would understand the law. Say some kid drops a bubble gum wrapper on the ground. It's his first offense. Ten years in jail. By the time he gets out, he's twenty years old. Say he's some real smarty-pants. Maybe the first chance he gets, he throws a beer can out the window. Second offense and zappo! It's the end for that guy. The town, go downstairs. It's right past the tax office before you get to "Men's."

Mom and Dad said the chief seemed kind of relieved to see them. There isn't much of a jail in our town. There's only this one section of the big police room that's kind of caged in. The chief hadn't put anyone in jail for so long that he was having difficulty finding the key. He asked my folks to guard the prisoner while he plowed through his desk drawers.

Naturally my parents wanted to get Abby out of there right away. The way they tell it, Miss Witherspoon just thanked them very much for coming. "No," she didn't want a lawyer. "No," she didn't want to be bailed out. The way she understood it she would have a hearing on Tuesday, and "yes," that suited her fine.

Finally Chief Tonioli gave up on finding the keys. It must have dawned on him that the lady he had arrested was no plain old crackpot. He was beginning to feel sheepish about the whole thing. He even asked Abby if maybe she was just playing a good-natured joke. Maybe they should just forget about the arrest and the fingerprints and the whole bit.

But Abby was determined to go the whole route. She told the chief she was arrested and intended to stay arrested. Chief Tonioli didn't really have any choice. Since she wasn't going to get herself bailed out or anything, and he couldn't find the keys to the town jail anyhow, he had to put handcuffs on her and drive her to the county jail!

The reporter from *The Evening Record* and Lisa Davidson, the editor of the high school paper, were on their way into Town Hall, when Abby, the chief, and my parents came piling through the doors. Honestly, it was almost like on T.V., except there should have been more reporters. But Lisa and that guy from the *Record* acted like big city pros! It's a shame they didn't have tape recorders and microphones and stuff, but they asked the same kind of questions the big shot reporters ask.

"Yes," she was going to plead guilty. She used bigger words and better English when she said it, but what she meant was Chief Tonioli was a symbol of a whole system that she was throwing water at. Maybe it was wrong to burn Taffy Teen Dolls without a permit, but who gave schools and the whole of everything a permit to squoosh girls? She went on and on, almost listing the ways girls got the short end of the stick. Her voice was different than before. It was slow and steady, the way Mrs. Martin gives a vocabulary test. "Ardently. He cheered the team ARDENTLY." The reporters were writing down every word she said.

I felt so mixed up. Jail was about the worst thing that could happen to anyone. But Miss Witherspoon, I mean Abby, looked happier than I had ever seen her. I couldn't believe she could look that happy. I mean, she held up her hands with the handcuffs right on them and made the V for victory sign! For a while I thought she had gone absolutely batty.

Dad seemed to read my mind. He put his arm

around my shoulder and told me not to worry about Miss Witherspoon. He said she knew just what she was doing. I could tell by the look in his eye that he was pretty amused.

I guess you think I'm a real birdbrain, but it took me all that time to realize what was happening: Abigail Witherspoon was putting it together for girls like it has never been put together before! I mean, everybody in the whole county reads the Sunday paper. If Abigail Witherspoon was going to jail, you can just bet everyone would think twice about why.

While Abby was climbing into Chief Tonioli's car, Jane started to cheer. We all picked it up as loud as we could: "Two, four, six, eight! Who do we appreciate?"

I mean Abby really was carrying the ball. She was really going to score for the girls' team! The only problem was where were the goalposts? Who decided that? Who was making the rules?

Aunt Francie says if the Women Libbers ever get what they want they'll be sorry. Oh wow, Aunt Francie! I hope you're wrong.

20

ALL DURING SUPPER I had this picture of Abby stuck in my head. I could just see her crouched in her cell, holding a hunk of stale bread and sipping water from a tin cup. She was wearing a striped suit like you have to in prison and a little round prison hat—but with a feather in it. Even if we weren't having Saturday Shipwreck, which is what David calls Mom's sweep-the-kitchen casseroles, I couldn't have eaten much. Not with that picture of Abby in my mind.

We were all kind of quiet during supper. Maybe we were just talked out. All afternoon people had been calling. My friends' parents called to talk with my parents. The radio station called to ask me a bunch of questions. Dorothy called. She had to have a whole conversation with Mom and David and me. Jibber-jabber. Yak-yak. Ugh!

Just when we smelled the rolls burning, the phone rang again. We all kind of groaned.

Guess who it was! It was the president of the

school board. He must have been just about the only person in town who hadn't heard about Miss Witherspoon. He had just gotten back from playing golf. From where I was sitting, I could see Dad smiling his company manners smile and asking those automatic questions adults ask each other.

Then Dad's expression changed. You know how these phony novelists are always saying, "Her face dropped when she saw the butler had become a werewolf"? Well, honestly, that's just what happened to my father's face. Maybe it didn't drop, but it sure drooped. He was saying, "I see" and "Thanks for letting me know." I couldn't figure out what was happening until Dad told us.

When he did tell us, I couldn't believe what he was saying. I mean how could she? The whole school board—well, just about the whole school board—had pretty much decided that Dad's plan for Woodbury Central was the best. But Abigail Witherspoon, rat-fink Benedict Arnold Witherspoon, had some "serious reservations." She questioned if an independent architect like Dad could handle a big project like building a school. I can just hear her lemonade voice icing up Dad's chances with the school board! She thought Dad's plan was better, "more imaginative," but wouldn't Calvert, Koch and Prendergast be better able to give "architectural supervision"? I mean who ran over to Town Hall to get her out of jail? If Calvert, Koch and Prendergast were such on-top-of-it guys, one of them could have at least showed up!

When Mom told Dad to remember Miss Witherspoon didn't actually have a vote, he told her to stop being Mary Poppins. Everything anybody wanted to say turned out to be the wrong thing. We just kind of all sat there, shuffling Saturday Shipwreck around on our plates.

I really jumped at the chance to escape when Julie called and asked if I could sleep over at her house. Mom and Dad said I could go and remember my manners and don't forget my toothbrush and get to bed at a reasonable hour. I disappeared with my sleeping bag before they could change their minds.

21

BY THE TIME I GOT to Julie's, Jane and Sam were there, and Suzy and Holly were on the way. See what I mean about stepmothers? All Julie probably said was, "Can I have a friend sleep over?"

"Have them all over. Have a slumber party!" That's what Julie's stepmother probably said.

We were all kind of excited to find ourselves together in the middle of a party. Sometimes if you have a few weeks to think about a party, when it finally comes off it's a drag. I mean you get thinking, wow, a party! It's going to be great! Then it turns out to be some kid's parents are trying to make you act like it's the nineteenth century and you have to play dumb party games instead of plain old games you like and you start having trouble talking to the same old kids you horsed around with yesterday.

Julie's party wasn't a bit like that. The moon was making it bright like day. Her folks said "sure," we could fool around outside. "Just stay in the neighborhood."

First we played tag. When we got tired of doing that, Suzy said we should be gathering clues to help defend Abby. None of us really believed that Abby needed us to "prepare the case," as Suzy said. It just fit in with our wacky mood to pretend we were detectives. We hid behind trees and pretended all station wagons were suspicious vehicles. We turned up our collars and called each other numbers like Agent 007. Except I was being a double agent. Abigail Witherspoon could get forty years at hard labor for all I cared!

Then Suzy got the idea that we should really go collect the Taffy Teen Dolls because they were honest-to-goodness evidence. Since we knew they wouldn't burn, Jane thought it was really gross to just leave them in the bonfire pit.

Jane is really freaky about the environment. Do you know what she wants? She wants them to give the death penalty for littering, second offense. Jane says the death penalty would stop littering right away.

It could start with ten-year-olds because any kid that big would understand the law. Say some kid drops a bubble gum wrapper on the ground. It's his first offense. Ten years in jail. By the time he gets out, he's twenty years old. Say he's some real smarty-pants. Maybe the first chance he gets, he throws a beer can out the window. Second offense and zappo! It's the end for that guy. The

Death Penalty. Don't you think that would be a rotten law, even if it did stop littering?

Anyhow, between Suzy wanting to gather evidence and Jane wanting to save the environment, we decided that what we had to do was get those Taffy Teen Dolls, or at least what was left of them.

Julie thought she ought to tell her folks where we were going. We could see them through the window. They had a fire going and were stretched out on the floor listening to some music. Can you imagine how it would sound if everyone in an orchestra was playing a broken electric appliance? Anyhow, I guess Julie's parents really like that kind of stuff. I mean, who was making them listen?

They looked so into the music, we decided not to disturb them. Besides, they might have said "no." We just took off.

We kind of ran, skipped, jogged, whirled, skittle-skooted towards Town Hall. We all felt—I don't know—kind of wacky and wonderful, like we had won the World Series or something.

We cut across the parking lot, hanging on to each others' shoulders and singing, "When the boys get in the way, we're gonna roll right over them." We were feeling so good, real winners.

Then someone focused a flashlight on the bonfire pit. All of a sudden we didn't feel like winners anymore.

22

"FREEZE!"

It was Chief Tonioli. He probably picked that up from some T.V. detective, but we froze just the same. He ran his big flashlight over us, back and forth and up and down. I can't tell you how rotten that made me feel. I mean I knew we weren't super-criminals or anything and getting a flashlight shined on you isn't like being stretched on the rack. It was almost like playing a part in a play, but still I felt awful. I don't know why, but I felt guilty. Isn't that dumb?

"O.K., you girls," the chief said. "Where are those dolls?"

We just looked at each other.

It was the creepiest! Someone had disappeared with all the Taffy Teen Dolls and fixed up a grave with a cross made out of popsicle sticks and a bunch of plastic flowers.

Yuk! My tummy was doing flip-flops again. The whole thing seemed kind of sick and twisted and dumb. How did I get into this mess in the first place? Suddenly I was mad. All the ginger ale bubbles, the silly-willy-goofy-good feelings were gone.

I could hear the police chief talking with the other kids. But all that was happening somewhere outside of me. My thoughts were all inside, going deeper and deeper, trying to connect with my feelings, until finally they bumped right into each other—whack! All the mix-ups and worrying, all the being uptight about meetings and having responsibilities that I didn't need suddenly were like flies buzzing around, looking for a place to land. And then they did land. They landed right on Mom.

I could hear Aunt Francie's arguments spinning away on my private record player. Policemen and Abigail Witherspoon and all the heavy things I've gotten mixed up with! If Mom was home being a "proper mother" like Aunt Francie said, would I have gotten into this whole mess in the first place? Being me used to be so easy!

"Meanwhile, back on the farm," Chief Tonioli was finally convinced that we weren't the ones who had taken the Taffy Teen Dolls. Somehow or other I found myself squeezed in the back seat of his car next to Sam. The chief was driving us all back to Julie's house, which was really pretty nice of him. There was still the feeling of a party, but somehow I wasn't with it.

It's funny how sometimes you can be right in the middle of all your friends and feel kind of alone. Once Suzy read me this poem she found. It said that no man is an island and all people are connected to each other. But somehow I had gotten loose, disconnected.

When the chief brought us back to Julie's house and everyone was sitting around the fire drinking mugs of hot chocolate and popping corn and wondering if we'd all have our pictures in the paper, there I was. The Island of Meg.

Oh wow! I didn't want to spend the night at Julie's or anybody else's. I wanted to go home. I wanted to be connected.

23

I TOLD EVERYONE THAT I thought I was coming down with something, a virus or even a light case of bubonic plague. I don't think Suzy believed me, but nobody was in the mood to give me truth serum.

Julie's father insisted on driving me home, even though their house is only three blocks away. But you know how parents are. They're always waiting for something horrible to happen to you.

Mom and Dad were half watching an old movie on T.V. Mom was lying on the floor, trying to make her toes touch behind her head. Dad was shuffling around the plans for the new school. I knew I wasn't interrupting some great film experience. To tell you the truth, I think that I would have interrupted anyhow.

Naturally they both wanted to know why I came home and was I sick. Mom was feeling my forehead and looking worried, and I began to feel more like a dope than an island! Just when I decided to fake a sick scene, which incidentally is no easy trick when your mother is a doctor, I remembered the way it was before with that flashlight all over me. I was angry all over again, all bubbles inside. Not soda pop bubbles but bad ones, like in a witch's cauldron.

"You don't want to be my mother," I said. "All you care about is Mrs. Gonzalez and a bunch of people that aren't even in your family."

Once I started I really got carried away! I told Mom how Aunt Francie was right. She did neglect us, and I probably would turn out to be a juvenile delinquent after all. Not that she'd care. It wasn't like I was one of her patients or anything.

To tell you the truth I was laying it on thick, and I kind of knew it too, deep down. I don't know why, but it was a crazy feeling. I could see I was really making an impression on my parents.

When David came bumbling home from Dorothy's house, he just stood there and looked at me. Then he asked what was going on and was I for real.

Then somehow, kerplunk, I slid off the broomstick and landed on my feet. I stopped. Just stopped. How had I ever gotten so carried away?

Mom looked pale and kind of old. I was noticing how the lines around her mouth just stayed there whether she was smiling or not.

Dad looked cool in a way I never saw before. I kind of half smiled at him. A kind of just-you-and-me-know smile. He didn't smile back.

I stood there and watched the water grow deeper and colder all around me. The land seemed farther away than ever. For a person who didn't want to be an island, I was sure burning bridges. I mean sure, I had been feeling angry and mixed up. But who did I expect to give me the Academy Award?

I wish that people came with big erasers. When you make a big scene and say a lot of stuff you don't really mean, you could rub it all off. Everything could be the way it was. But people don't come that way.

Dad said that if I was finished, I had better sit down. Sit down! I felt like disappearing down a hole for a few dozen years, but I sat down anyhow.

Dad asked me if I wanted to say anything. I wanted to say I'm sorry, but the words turned to peanut butter. I just shook my head.

"Then I want you to listen to me and think about what I'm saying, Meg."

He didn't shout or anything. I just knew he meant business. I don't remember exactly what he said, but I was reaching. Reaching out of me. Reaching for his words and holding onto them.

The thing about the way they talk, my parents, is they talk with you, not at you the way some adults do. Like Mrs. Martin, my teacher, her words come at you ak-ak-ak. You feel like a duck in a shooting gallery. That makes you want to get inside a bulletproof vest or something.

Dad said he guessed I had been feeling pretty angry. It's funny. I wasn't feeling angry anymore. Just a little bit empty.

And all the things I had said to Mom, all those

things, they were like bullets. But Mom isn't a wooden duck. She's people like I'm people. She has her own feelings. I didn't need to say I was sorry for having hurt them. She already knew I was. She kind of slipped her arm around me and gave me a mini-squug. The space between us wasn't so far, anymore.

Dad said that the people who try to change things have to take some risks. I think that was the word he used, risks. Deep down I'm not sure I want to take risks. I'm not really sure if I'm a go-alonger or a changer or a stay-the-samer.

One thing I'll never understand is the way Dad stuck up for Abby. If they ever print another volume of the Bible, THE VERY NEW TESTAMENT, or something, they should get my father to write it. They really should. He knows how to turn the other cheek like a pro.

You probably won't believe this, but he isn't mad at Abigail Witherspoon! Not one little bit. He said all that Abby had done was give a "non-emotional, intelligent opinion."

"So how can I be angry?" he asked. "Disappointed, yes, but not angry."

Honestly! Wouldn't you be fuming? I mean a friend shouldn't be giving "non-emotional, intelligent opinions," unless they're the right opinions! A friend should be on your side all the time. If someone wanted me to give a "non-emotional, intelligent opinion" about one of my friends, do you know what I'd say? Go ask a machine! That's what!

But Dad, he said honesty is probably the most important quality a friend can have. I guess I'd put loyalty on the top of my list, but I don't know. It wouldn't do you much good to have a loyal liar for a friend.

That's just one more thing I don't know. There's so much I don't know, I can't even figure out where to start.

Mom said that the most important thing to know is who you are. I guess maybe I'm just beginning to find out who I am. It takes time to get it all together. Just when you think you have all the pieces in the right place, something slips and you have to put it together a new way.

One thing I know for sure. I've done enough looking for one day. I'm even too tired to stay mad at Abigail Witherspoon.

After all, even though tomorrow's Sunday, I'm not exactly going to sleep late. In just a few hours the morning papers will be out. Abby's picture will probably be smack on the first page. Jane and Suzy and Sam and Julie, all the Saturday Sisters, we'll probably all be there!

The thing is—after tomorrow, nothing is going to be quite the same in this town again. I mean just you wait till they read what we have to say! Just you wait!

ABOUT THE AUTHOR

Bobbi Katz lives in the Hudson Valley with her husband and two children, Joshua and Lori, only a few miles away from where she was born and spent her childhood.

While majoring in the History of Art at Goucher College, she wrote a catalog raisonée for the Baltimore Museum of Art on Matisse's first illustrated book. She became acquainted with the beautiful "livres de luxe" that outstanding artists were creating in limited editions.

After haunting New York City as a ghost writer on the Middle East, she attended Hebrew University in Israel.

As her own family grew up, she became involved with illustrated books again—not the rare editions for museums, but books for children.

Bobbi Katz is the author of two picture books —*Nothing But a Dog* and *I'll Build My Friend a Mountain*—and a book of poetry called *Upside Down and Inside Out*.